I Am

Corey Wolff

ISBN 978-1-7337892-8-8 (paperback)

For Bella and Caleb

Always remember that your biggest challenges were given by G-d so you can discover the greatness that is already within you.

I Am

by

Corey Wolff

Transcendence Press

The wound is the place where the light

enters you.

Rumi

Chapter 1

The I Am believed itself to be a salmon. And so it was a salmon. It had undergone a difficult journey, struggling against the current for many days and not eating since it entered the stream. Now, with chunks of missing skin which had stopped healing, and beset with white fungus eating away its flesh, it had grown tired, tired of swimming upstream, tired of sacrificing its life for reasons that seemed to have no meaning. Unsure of what it wanted, feeling empty and lost inside, it knew it was not being true to itself. With each waterfall it traversed it had become more disheartened, and with each passing day it became wearier and more beaten from following a path which it did not believe was its own. Yet, the I Am continued to move with the herd. And as it did, other salmon pushed past it, eager to get ahead.

"Why am I fighting my way upstream," asked the I Am.

"So you can bring more salmon into the world," said the others.

"But this journey is killing me," the I Am responded. "Why must I put myself through all this pain? And is it worth it? My children will be alone, with no one to encourage or guide them on their journey. They will never learn to develop their own dreams, and like me, they will follow the same path of misery. There has to be more to life than this."

"Salmon don't have their own dreams!" said the others. "Salmon don't question why they return to the place of their birth! They must follow the herd."

"But why have we traveled for our entire lives, merely to end up in the same place we have begun?" said the I Am.

The others did not respond. Instead they tenaciously plodded against the current, believing they were heroes, sacrificing themselves so their offspring could continue. But the I Am began to wonder if they were really fools. Both a hero and a fool sacrifice their lives, but a fool is convinced that the sacrifice has meaning when there isn't one. What meaning is there in a life without the pursuit of a dream? Then the I Am thought, "Maybe they are just cowards who have never found the courage to dream." Yet, it was also following the others. Maybe it was just as much a fool, or a coward.

As the I Am surmounted yet another waterfall, it witnessed the salmon next to it jump directly into the gaping maw of a grizzly bear, watching in horror as the animal began to peel off the skin and rip open the carcass. At first it wanted to erase this brutality from its mind. But then it began to think it could use this as an opportunity to speak to a creature outside of the herd, and since the bear seemed content with its fresh kill, the I Am did not need to worry about being eaten. So it turned around, swimming to the bear who was now on the bank of the river. As it feasted on its dinner, the I Am, lifting its head from the water, asked, "Bear, please tell me, why am I fighting to make my way upstream?"

The bear slowly chewed on the soft flesh, and then looked into the eyes of the I Am, never having an idea that it was merely looking at another expression of itself. "Bears need to eat salmon for the land to be filled with life. If salmon didn't make their way upstream, I would not be able to feed myself, and the cubs of other bears would go hungry. We would no longer fertilize the soil. Plants, flowers, and trees would not have the nutrients to grow. That would affect many species which live close to the river. Salmon, in order for life to exist, you must go upstream!"

"It all works out for you," said the I Am, "but not for that salmon who is being eaten. I think it would regret its choice."

"But plenty of salmon do make it to their destination," the bear added, "and they produce many offspring which sustain life for the entire forest. Why are you so miserable?"

The I Am replied, "Because even if I am successful, my children will never learn to develop their own dreams, and like me, they will follow the same path of misery. I am not sure what I should do. I have never learned to have trust in my own decisions."

"And why is that?" asked the bear.

"It began when I was young, living within the gravel of the river bottom," said the I Am. "Often, I would see a glimmering light from above, and I would wonder what was out there. Then one day I heard a voice. 'Come to me!' it said.

" 'Who are you?' I asked.

" 'It is me,' the voice responded. 'I have come to protect you. I will show you the ways of the world and give you knowledge of everything in all the waters.'

"I thought this was my father who had finally come for me," the I Am continued. "When I left the safety of the gravel, I was surprised to see many others who had been lured away from the darkness. And there was a long figure writhing above with a shimmering light around it. As the others approached, the beast gulped them down. And as they struggled to get out, they pushed against its insides, their heads protruding against its soft underbelly.

The bear, who had stopped eating because she was immersed in the I Am's story said, "That sounds terrifying. How did you escape?"

"I quickly tried to hide," said the I Am. "I could not go back to where I had lived for all my young life or else I would be engulfed by the beast. So I swam as far as I could and hid under a fallen log.

"I had no parents to teach me how to protect myself, no idea which creatures I could trust, and I stayed hidden, scared to risk being exposed, burying my head to the world. Eventually, as I grew larger my hunger compelled me to leave the river bottom and enter the sea. There, I along with other salmon banded together to survive, following each other's movements to maintain the illusion of one consciousness. When a salmon close to me moved suddenly, I followed, because there was safety in numbers. For we had to pretend we were all one enormous entity. Moving with the herd in the vast expanse of the ocean helped me cover great distances and travel to places I never thought possible. Everything I have accomplished has been because of the herd. But it has been a large price to pay. All this time, I have remained with salmon for protection, yet none of my decisions have been my own."

"I see why you haven't been able to trust yourself and others. I have also found it difficult to trust," said the bear. "Although I was raised by my mother, I longed to meet my father, and hoped that one day he would return." The bear began to share her memories of when she was a cub, memories so strongly etched into her psyche, that the thought made her relive them.

"One day I asked my mother, 'Where is my dad? Why is he not with us? What did we do wrong to make him leave?'

"'My sweet cub, you have done nothing wrong,' my mother responded, as she nuzzled her snout against my cheek, 'Your dad and I were together for a short time. And that time had a purpose, which was to bring you and your brothers into the world. I don't know where your father is. But I thank God every day for blessing me with all of you.' After that, I never expected to meet my father, and I was at peace with having only our mother raise us.

"Then one day an enormous lumbering creature emerged at the top of the river bank, and its foreboding shadow cast down upon us. Our father had returned, but he was not the loving and nurturing soul whom I imagined," the bear said, as she recalled the source of her trauma. "When my father saw me and my brothers, he became enraged. My oldest brother said, 'Father, I love you. Now we can be together as a family.' But as he sprinted over to greet him, our father struck, his powerful claws leaving an enormous gash in his head, killing him instantly. I was able to climb a tree and escape, but I could only stare in horror and disbelief as my own father murdered my entire family, tearing apart my mother as she tried to protect her boys, and then killing my brothers, tearing off their skin, and eating their flesh. How could God allow this to happen? My brothers and my mother were innocent and good. What purpose could this serve?

"For the first time in my life, I was alone," she told the I Am. "In shock, I stared for a while at the water as it flowed downstream. Then I bawled from the loss of my family and moaned to withstand the pangs of hunger. To survive, I mostly foraged for berries, and caught salmon as they made their way up the river. I don't know why God would make creatures who murder their young. But bears are all capable of inflicting such misery. As I have grown, I learned that suffering is a part of life. To survive, I had to endure it; to keep existing, and provide for my cubs, I needed to be the cause of it.

"I wanted to avoid the mistakes my mother made and choose a spouse who is gentle and kind, but I was drawn to the same type of male as her. When I had cubs, my husband abandoned us. I tried to be a good parent, and teach my cubs the ways of the forest. And life seemed to go on. Just when I thought they would never see their father again, he returned. But once he saw how important my cubs were to me, he became enraged with jealousy, and murdered my son before my eyes. I do not know the point of my suffering. No matter how much I loved my cubs, I was not able to protect them from their own father," said the bear. "I do not have the answers you seek."

Filled with shame, the bear hanged her head down and continued to pick at her dinner. The I Am felt sad for the bear, and also for itself. It wanted to comfort it, but it had no idea what to say. It seemed there were also creatures who were much bigger and more powerful who could not escape life's misery and made the same mistakes as those that came before them.

Chapter 2

Feeling more lost than before, the I Am continued its journey. Eventually it saw a group of eagles, a larger one with white plumage on its head along with several fledglings tearing into a fresh kill along the river bank. It swam up to the eagle father and asked, "What is the point of all the pain and suffering I have to experience? Why must I condemn my little ones to the same life of misery as I have endured?"

The eagle father told the I Am, "If salmon didn't try to return to their birthplace, there would be nothing to eat for my young ones. Then they would never become strong."

"Yes, that is true," said the I Am, "But those that make the journey would still be alone and have no one to guide them. Most would still have offspring which are devoured by predators. Why should salmon bring lives into existence only to cause them pain?"

The eagle picked at the lifeless fish in front of him, then said, "Salmon, I have also asked myself why life is filled with pain. And when I was young, I also felt alone and had no one to guide me." Then the eagle began to think back, recalling the deeply embedded memories of its early life.

"When my brother and I were just eaglets, our parents would leave us alone while they hunted for prey. One time a large raven invaded our nest. The raven, landing right next to us, lunged at my brother, but I pushed him out of the way before the beast, thrusting its sharp beak at his eyes and throat, made contact with his delicate flesh. It grabbed hold of me, and as it began to drag me away, I let out a shriek, for I was fearful I would be killed and eaten. Suddenly, my father swooped down and pierced his claws into its flesh, ripping out its viscera. I watched in shock as life faded from its eyes. 'Don't be scared my eaglets. This is the way of the world. If I did not kill this creature, it would have killed one of you.'

"'I knew you would protect us,' I said.

"'Of course,' my father replied. 'I will always be here for my sweet eaglets.' Then my brother and I nuzzled against him, feeling the warmth of his body as we fell asleep. I remember the next morning, watching in amazement as his massive frame cast a shadow over us. And I remember the last time I saw him. Standing at the edge of the nest, he said, 'I'll see you soon, my little eaglets.' Just then, I felt a raindrop land on my tiny beak, and I was filled with fear as I saw storm clouds gather.

"'Please don't go,' I pleaded to my father, my voice trembling. 'It's not safe to hunt in a storm.'

"'I have to find food for you. I will be back soon,' my father said. Soon after he left, there was an enormous storm. But I knew my father was strong. Many days passed, yet my brother and I remained hopeful he would return.

"I often remembered the times my brother and I had spent with him, sharing all the places we would explore when we were old enough. Sometimes I heard him say, 'I'll always be with you, my eaglets.' But when I turned towards the voice, there was nothing. And when I called out to him, I was answered only by the taunting howl of the wind.

"As I became a fledgling, my curiosity about the world continued to grow. Although I wanted to explore the wilderness, my eagle mother insisted on us staying in the nest and feeding us like little eaglets, placing carrion from her beak into our mouths. I hated the putrid smell of rotting meat surrounded by swarming insects, and would gag on the writhing larvae as I was forced to gulp it down.

"Then, one day, my mother said, 'Your father is dead. He was weak and didn't survive the storm.'

"'That is a lie. He will come back,' I said. But my mother smugly lifted her beak and turned away."

"Your mother was not able to connect with you," said the I am, captivated yet saddened by the story of the eagle's early life. "That must have been hard."

"It was very difficult," said the eagle. "And her words stirred up both anger and fear deep within me. In fact, that night I had a terrible dream, a dream of my father soaring below the storm clouds, watching, waiting to see movement on the ground. When he noticed a mink running frantically, he swooped down with an unearthly quickness. And as he approached, he was suddenly struck by a bolt of lightning. As he plummeted toward the earth, I awoke screaming. It rained and thundered, and the wind whistled all around me and my brother as we huddled in the corner of the nest.

"'Mom, I need you,' I cried out.

"But she raised her eyelid and squawked, 'Stop crying. You are selfish for waking me up.' Then she went back to sleep.

"The next day, when my mother returned from hunting, she was happier than I had ever seen her. As she arrived, a fox jumped inside the nest from a nearby branch. 'Fox will now be living with us,' she said.

"'I am excited to eat you, uh, I mean meet you,' said the fox, as he licked his lips.

"I looked at my mother and responded, 'How well do you know this fox? How can we trust him?'

"'What do you know about life?' she said, annoyed that I questioned her. 'You are just a little eaglet. This fox gives me attention and makes me feel special,' said my eagle mother. And he will be a good father to both of you.'

"The fox and my eagle mother would often bring back rotting meat, and it would stop our tiny stomachs from rumbling. Although it relieved us of hunger, I remembered how my eagle father despised eating carrion and preying upon scavengers who ate decayed flesh. The values we had seemed to be lost with my father's absence, and with no one to stick to them, they didn't appear to matter.

"Eventually, the fox began to scare us. He would stare and me and my brother, lick his lips and say, "Let me nibble on your necks, so I can taste the sweetness of fresh meat.'

"'Please don't eat us,' I said, terrified.

"'Well, just let me chew on your legs,' said the fox. "A few bites is all I need. Let me munch on your little wings so I can feel how tender they are.'

"'No,' I said. 'Leave us alone. Mom, help! Help! This creature wants to eat us.'

"'That's ridiculous,' she said. 'Fox is helping me to provide for you. You are an ungrateful bird,' she said. But the fox's craving for the taste of a fresh kill only increased.

"One night we were awakened by the fox's growl and the sound of my mother's flapping wings followed by her high-pitched scream. Then she shouted, 'Get off me. Please help me, my eaglets.'

"Terrified, we hid our faces, curled up against the side of the nest, clutching each other. I knew we did not belong with these creatures. I just wanted our eagle father to take us away from this place.

"'I'm scared,' my brother said.

"I called out, 'Where are you dad? We need you. Please come and take us away.' But there was just emptiness. And then I felt my brother being torn from me, and heard his high pitched whistling as the fox tried to drag him away into the darkness. 'Hold onto me,' I said.

"'Please don't let me go,' he said.

"I held onto my brother as tight as I could, but the fox jerked his head violently, with jaws clamping down on his neck until he broke free of my grip. And the fox carried away my brother into the dark night.

"Exhausted and shocked by what took place, I stared at the stars gleaming in the clear night sky, wondering if my father would ever return. And when I scanned the nest, droplets of my brother's blood on the floor seeped into my awareness that I was the only fledgling who remained. I looked again into the abyss of the night sky, consumed by desolation and immersed in melancholy. My eagle mother said, 'Forget about what is beyond the nest. You must stay here where you will be safe and protected.'

"'Protected? You have not protected us. You have destroyed us. You have brought a fox into our home who shook my brother by the head until his neck broke and then ran off with his jaws holding his limp body.'

"Then her eyes began to well up with tears. And with a hateful look on her face, she said, 'You're ungrateful for all I've sacrificed for you. If you were strong enough, your brother would still be alive. You've always been weak.'

"As much as I despised her, I believed her words were true. I tried to hold onto him, but I couldn't do it. After the time my brother was taken, I struggled each day of my life, knowing I was the one to blame. And there was a piece of my soul which was missing.

"One day, after my mother finished feeding me from her beak she said, 'Tell me how grateful you are to be with me. Tell me how special I am and what a good mother I have been to you. Tell me how lucky you are to have me sacrifice my life to raise you.'

"'I don't think you are special,' I said. 'You are a cruel creature who has made me your prisoner. All I wanted was to learn to be strong, so I could live my own life. But you have taken that from me.'

"Then filled with anger, she squawked, 'I want you out of this nest. Remember this day. It is the day I disown you. You are no longer my little eaglet.

Let's see how well you do without me.'
Not knowing what else to do, I hopped onto the branch of a tree, huddled against the trunk, anxious about being able to fend for myself in the world."

The eagle then flapped its wing a few times, and gulped down another piece of flesh from the salmon it stood upon. Looking at the I Am, he said, "If you asked me then about the purpose of suffering, I would have said there is none. If I had a mother who treated me with love, I would have had a more rewarding life. If I had a father who was present, I would have learned to hunt and how to provide for myself.”

“What changed?” asked the I am, filled with anticipation.

“That night, as I perched on that branch, I had another dream. I was on a mountain top, and as I heard the whistling of the wind all around me, I saw my eagle father. He opened his wings,and when the air current lifted him off the ground effortlessly, he said, ‘Fly with me!’

“ ‘I can’t!’ I replied hopelessly. ‘My brother is dead because I wasn’t strong enough to protect him. I can never be a mighty eagle like you. I am sorry that I am such a disappointment,' I said as I hung my head in shame.

"'You are not to blame for what happened,' said my eagle father. 'There was no one to protect you both. The world has convinced you that you are powerless. But that is not true. You are the one who controls your destiny.'

"Then I awoke," said the eagle. "As I looked down, I became aware of my strong frame and powerful wings, the sharpness of my long-curved beak, and thick hooked talons which could tear into flesh. I then realized what had been limiting me was my belief in myself. Although I was scared, I was determined to take the leap, for I knew it was the beginning of the creation of a new life. But just as I opened my wings, I felt something grab my leg. As I plummeted toward the ground, I was shocked to learn its source. It was my mother.

"She said, 'You can't leave me!' I believed she would destroy both of us, so I clamped down on her with my beak. As she released her grip, she shed several feathers from her lacerated hide. 'Please!' she squawked, as blood trickled from the gash on her chest. 'Without you, I don't know who I am.'

"Salmon, it was then I understood she had taken from me in order to have what she could not find within herself. She had an emptiness within her own heart, which could not be filled. Although I felt sorry for her because of her limitations, limitations which gave her a need for having control rather than a desire to develop a loving connection, I was still determined to finally give myself what I needed, my freedom."

"'I hope you can find a way to love yourself. But I won't sacrifice my life for you,' I said to my eagle mother. Then I flew away, and as I ventured into the great unknown, I never looked back. As time went on, I came to understand that my suffering had been necessary to develop the character to persevere through those challenges. I needed to understand the pain of being stifled, so I would never do that to my own eaglets, so I could prepare them to be strong.

"Now that I am a parent," the eagle continued, "I can encourage them to fly on their own and to develop the skills they will need to lead independent lives. With each day, I choose to be better than the parent I was given. I choose to be thoughtful and kind. I choose to listen to what they need. As I respond to them in each moment, I choose who I wish to become.

"Salmon, suffering may seem to be a punishment, but it is really a gift to help you to discover the purpose that God has for you. God puts challenges in your life, so you can use them as opportunities for your own growth. But it is your responsibility to face them. It is God testing you, to see if you will give up and accept the belief that you are helpless or if you will strive to direct the course of your own destiny.

The I Am then asked, "But how do I direct my own life when every salmon in the herd tells me to follow them?"

The eagle felt the cool water moving past his talons and the gentle breeze against his feathers while he stood along the riverbank. "Do not listen to those from the herd tell you who you are, for they know not what is inside of you. When you hear their voice for long enough, you come to believe it is your own that is speaking. But it is an illusion.

It is the voice of others which has taken over your mind. When you follow that voice, you fail to honor yourself. You move against the current of love. You lose your connection to the divinity within you. Love yourself enough to ignore the voice of others, and listen to your own. For it is only when you truly honor and love yourself that you change the destiny of your children."

"But salmon don't get the chance to raise their young," expressed the I Am. "Most of us die shortly after we bury our eggs in the river bottom."

The eagle responded, "You still have it within you to direct the course of your own destiny. It is your choice to follow those that came before you. It is your choice to move on the same path as those who are next to you. And it is your choice to bring about life which will experience hardship as you have." The I Am admired the eagle for what it had accomplished, but it did not believe these were choices which it could make. After all, it was a salmon, not an eagle. It wondered if there was another way besides family life for a soul to purify itself.

Chapter 3

Still, something within the I Am had begun to change. Now it moved through the water aimlessly. A little girl watching from the river bank noticed that it seemed to have no direction at all. "Why aren't you swimming upstream?" said the girl. "Are you sick?" And she slowly extended her hand so the I Am could rub against it. As her fingers entered the water, the I Am looked up, and noticed they appeared to bend slightly at the surface. "How could this be?" thought the I Am. "Is everything within the stream an illusion? Perhaps the world above isn't real." It began to wonder what prevented it from seeing the truth, to wonder if its entire life had been nothing but a dream. After all, it didn't remember all the years of its life when it was in the ocean. It had glimpses of its past, bubbles which would rise to the surface of its consciousness. But it could not remember much of its journey. Despite this, the I Am loved the attention from the girl. And when they touched, it felt complete.

"Come with me. I'll take care of you, and feed you every day, and you'll be mine," said the girl. The I Am agreed.

Finally, it was able to leave the river and receive the nurturing it had always craved. She brought it home, and placed it in her fish tank. Once the water was still, the I Am began to feel a rhythmic thumping which gradually became louder. It wondered what its source could be. It also felt the walls of hard glass against its body, through which it looked out at a world it could not be a part of. Again, feeling empty and without purpose, it found itself living a life it did not want, and it quickly came to understand that it was in a prison of its own making. It craved the sound of water rushing past it and feeling the power of the current against its scales.

The I Am soon realized it needed to be back in nature. Time seemed to stand still in the tank, and it began to wonder if it would ever be free. It wondered how it repeatedly found itself entangled in a life of misery. Each time it felt the walls of the glass prison, it became more disheartened, eventually just floating on its side, occasionally moving its fins.

"Stop floating! You need to swim. That's what makes me happy," said the girl as she placed her hands on her hips.

But then she began to wonder if the salmon was truly sick. So she dropped a pebble into the tank and pressed her cheek up against the glass, her eye carefully watching for signs of movement. As the stone plummeted toward the sandy bottom and the I Am watched the ripple expand across the water's surface, it could not help but wonder how its life was much like that ripple. It had no one to guide it on making its own choices; it could not protect itself, and it lived in fear of being eaten. And those experiences which had begun as a tiny ripple, expanded over time. It was the reason it was too scared to leave the herd, even though there was no room for it to make its individual decisions about its own life. It was the reason it looked for something outside of itself to make its life better. That tiny ripple had led the I am to where it was. It wondered why the other salmon also did not end up in this tank. It knew that it was different somehow. Unlike the others, it knew its path had not been the right one.

Eventually, the girl could no longer stand it. "You are so ungrateful. I give you a beautiful tank to swim in, but you just lay on your side. I talk to you, but you give me no attention. You are the worst pet I have ever had," she said. Then she put the I Am back into a bucket which she wheeled in a tiny wagon toward the stream. When she was close, she spilled the bucket onto the slope of the river bank. But the I Am did not enter the water. Instead, it remained in the dirt, flopping against the ground, gasping frantically as the girl, not bothering to turn around, pulled her little wagon back up the hill. The I Am again felt the rhythmic thumping which increased as it tried to push water through its gills, but the more it gasped, the weaker it became.

The I Am continued to struggle for its life as more members of the herd passed by. "We told you not to leave us," they said. And they were happy they had all stuck together and kept swimming against the current because they believed they were right to be afraid of the unknown. The I Am's gasping became less frequent and intense. It wished it could have done more with its life, but now it was too late. The thumping became weaker until it stopped. It was no longer able to feel its tail. Then it could not feel its body at all. It could do nothing but stare at the brightness of the sun.

Eventually it began to feel a warmth enveloping it. It wondered if it could move, and when it looked down it saw that it no longer had a tail, but two legs. It then noticed that it no longer had fins, but arms. And suddenly, it felt it's face, and it was not the face of a fish, but that of a human. It became aware that it was no longer struggling to move its gills and gasping for life, but calmly breathing air from above the surface. And it realized it was not in the mud of the river bank, but on a rock seeing the light of the sun glimmer on the running water. Then the salmon saw a radiant and luminous light blue skinned figure at the mouth of a cave in a cross legged sitting posture facing him. "Where am I?" said the I am.

"Everywhere," said the figure.

"But who are you, and what do you want from me?"

"Identity is only a veil. There exists only truth, the essence of divine consciousness," said the figure.

"I am not sure what you mean," said the I am.

The blue figure replied, "Sometimes this consciousness communicates through dreams or visions; sometimes it is a feeling that speaks from within. It has been called many names, but it is The One That Brings Forth into Existence the Seen from That Which Is Unseen. It is both the Creator of the Universe and its creation."

"I don't understand what you mean," said the I Am. But the figure did not speak. Instead it slowly pointed to a spider's web which gleamed from the light of the sun. A female black widow mated with a male, and then, spinning her silk, wrapped him up into a cocoon. Then she began sucking out his insides.

The I Am asked, "How can the world allow such things? Why would the Creator bring a creature into existence whose purpose is to be eaten by his mate?"

And the blue figure said, "But that is not the purpose of his soul. Before, that black widow was in the form of a man. And as a man, he abused many women. So his soul has returned to this world as a spider who must be victimized and make his mate strong to help her survive. He must feel all the pain he caused others. For that is the only way his soul can fulfill the debt of his karma. Karma is much like the web of a spider. With each intention, thought, and action we take, we further entangle ourselves. Just as each strand of karma is woven, so it must be unwoven, until it is free.”

“How can the strands be unwoven?” asked the I Am.

“Only man can break the grip of his karma,” said the manifestation. So the I Am had much to think about. It wondered what its reason was for being born a salmon. It also wondered if it even was a salmon, since it now seemed to have a human body. Had it been alive before? What else had it been? Why had it been born? What did its soul have to learn?

"Please tell me, am I a salmon dreaming that I am a man, or am I a man who has dreamt he is a salmon," said the I Am.

The blue figure responded, "Your senses have given you the illusion that you are these things. You are not a man, nor are you a salmon. But you are in a dream - a dream within the mind of God, a consciousness which has forgotten it is dreaming. Just as each life you encounter in your own dreams is an expression of yourself, you are an expression of the Creator. You are a divine particle in a neural pathway of an infinitely expanding consciousness."

"I am not sure I understand," said the I Am. "I just want my life to be more than following what others expect. I want my life to be more than an endless cycle of misery. I want the power to choose my own destiny. I want to be a man."

The blue figure sat quietly, taking a long pause, and then extended his index finger, pointing to a swarm of ants in the dirt moving in a large swirling vortex. "Each ant in this colony is blind, and relies on the others by following their scent," said the figure. "Sometimes an ant will become lost. When it wanders back to the others, the ants all follow the new trail, spiraling around until they die.

"Why are you showing me this?" said the I am.

"Much like the ants caught in an unbreakable loop, many men follow the same path as those who came before them."

"Why do they do that?" asked the I am.

"Because they are attracted to what feels familiar. But this is what causes them to imprison themselves. Even worse, they set their own children on the same path.

"But you said man can break the grip of his karma. So how does he do that?" asked the I am.

"Unlike these ants, man is not blind," said the blue figure. "If he opens his eyes, he can see where his behavior will lead. He does not have to follow those who came before him, because has free will. Man can choose his destiny. Each person has it within him to forge a new path. But very few do, because the desire to follow the familiar is so strong. Yet, it can be done.

The blue figure continued, "Man is special because he is made in the likeness of The Creator. Just as consciousness uses its will to create the universe, man can use his will to create the life he desires. Through the power of his belief, he can bring what he imagines into existence. Man has the power to control his thoughts. This allows him to direct his own destiny. However, during a man's life, he often does not develop the awareness he has such power. To live is to dream. Most men never truly dream, and so they never truly live. But for the man who dreams, endless possibilities bloom, and the universe welcomes him.

"What about me?" said the I am. "Is it possible to choose my own destiny?"

"Rarely it is possible for another creature to dream, and thereby to choose its own destiny, if its will is strong," said the blue figure.

"Please make me a human," said the I Am.

"As a human, you would forget that your soul had chosen to return. And you would forget the potential you have to bring forth what you imagine into existence. By becoming human, it would be up to you to discover the divine seed inside you, to nurture it, and to bring it forth into the world. When man discovers his purpose, he connects to the divinity within him and expresses the glory of God on Earth.

"Why does man have this divine seed?" asked the I Am.

"It is divine consciousness wishing to awaken by sowing itself within the heart of man. It begins to awaken when it looks at itself and sees the reflection of its divinity. That only happens when one lives his purpose.”

“But how does man come to know his purpose?” asked the I Am.

“When man strives to help others solely because it nurtures his own heart, without expecting anything in return, that is when he lives his purpose. By realizing the greatest difficulties and struggles which have been placed before him have been placed there by his creator so he can grow, he begins to discover the meaning he creates for his own life. When he boldly faces these difficulties, it points him in the direction he is meant to take, to be the person he is meant to become. Man is tested by the Creator of the universe with each challenge put in front of him. And man discovers his purpose when each challenge stokes the burning flame of desire inside of him to strive to overcome, to refuse to accept defeat, and continue on, until he reaches his dream. When man can say that he did not choose his purpose, rather, his purpose chose him, that is when he knows the reason for his journey on Earth.

And when man does not find his purpose, he is much like a salmon fighting his way upstream, following the mad herd which discourages him from learning who he is. The majority of men might just as well be salmon, for they follow a path which dishonors themselves, and which discourages their children, and their species from evolving spiritually," the blue figure lamented, highlighting the plight of those swimming against the current, souls entirely disconnected from the oneness of the universe.

"I am ready to find my purpose," said the I Am.

"You are not yet ready, my child. The burdens you carry have kept you from growing. Speak aloud the source of this pain."

And the I Am, hesitant to express itself, began to have its eyes well up with tears. Then it said, "My wound is from my father who was not there to protect me when I needed him. I have always been alone. I have had to raise myself and the world has only tried to take from me. I don't know what I am supposed to do with my life," said the I am.

"I know you are afraid," said the blue figure. "But it is only when you let go of your attachments to the past that you can begin to feel your connection to all that is."

"I have held onto my pain for so long, I don't know who I am without it. I'm scared to let it go," said the I Am.

"To grow, my child, you must confront your fear of the unknown. When you have faith, anything becomes possible, because you experience the kingdom of heaven within you.

And the I Am began to understand that through faith in itself, it could direct the course of its destiny. No longer would it be enslaved by the expectations of others; no longer would it succumb to their will. It understood it could trust itself, do what it felt was right, and begin to unravel itself from the cycle in which it was trapped. It began to know who it was.

"I am the creator of my own life," said the I am. "Then, as the mouth of the cave slowly turned to the side, the I Am noticed an enormous eye. It realized it was not an opening to a cave at all, but the mouth of a fish.

Then the I Am sensed this creature's thoughts enter its mind. "I have been observing your life," said the enormous salmon. "I have always wished I could protect you, and that I could have given you the love you needed.

"What are you?" asked the I am.

"I am your father," it said.

"Why did you bring me into the world?" said the I Am. "I needed you to protect me, but all I found was emptiness."

Then the I Am's fish father said, "My son, I had only known what was given to me. For I was also left all alone. I spent my time fighting against the current. It was not until the end of my journey when I realized my goals had not been my own, for I had been misled, and it was my fault for listening to the others. I had struggled to get ahead, chasing the promise that I would be happy one day. But my happiness never came, and when I reached the mating pool where I was born, it was filled with salmon, many of them no longer teaming with life. Like me, they once had greatness inside them which was never realized because they had never given themselves the chance to have their own dreams. After I was able to spawn, I looked around, seeing birds pecking out the remaining eyeballs of the dead, and hearing flies buzzing as they laid eggs in the decaying flesh of those from the herd.

I discovered that I was out of time, and had made no progress on my journey. I wondered how many generations of salmon before me followed the same path, starting with no one to protect them and going through their entire lives only to learn that they had been wasted. I did the best I could based on what I knew. I am so sorry I was not there to protect you.

Then the I Am placed its hand on the head of his salmon father and caressed him." I know how you have struggled," the I Am said. "The pain you caused me was because of the pain in your own heart, and for that I forgive you!"

Then the I Am swum past the blue radiant and luminous being into the mouth of the fish father, and, still in the form of a human, reached into the viscera and pulled out the beating heart. As he held it in his hands, he saw several arrows which were impaled in the muscle. He broke off the tip of each, then pulled the shafts embedded in the thick muscular tissue completely and let them fall away. As the I Am began to feel the strength and steady rhythmic beating of the heart, it pushed it back into the viscera, then swam out from the mouth of the fish father. Even though it moved farther away, it heard the beating of the heart grow louder. "Salmon, speak now what it is you found," said the voice of That Which is Greater.

"I learned that by healing the heart of another, I also heal my own," said the I Am.

"You are beginning to feel the connection which exists between all things."

"How is that connection possible?" asked the I Am.

"Because all things are an illusion. There is only one thing. And you are an expression of that one thing, the mind of God, divine consciousness healing itself."

Epilogue

A feeling of serenity now pulsed within the I Am, as it slowly began to awaken. The hard rain had caused mud to slide down the wall of the river bank, and it had carried the I Am back into the stream. It remembered when it was in the ocean long ago, swimming with many others to create the illusion they were all one being. Now it realized it was no illusion, that each salmon was an expression of the Creator, attuned to the source of all things. But its soul had become out of harmony with the universe once it decided to follow the others up stream. Now, it noticed the water flowing around the rocks, rocks whose surface had become smooth from many years of the gentle flowing of the river. And the I Am, with renewed strength from the water going through its gills, decided to move with the current, following the voice from within. "I will become that which I choose to become," it said.

Once it believed it was a fish on a journey throughout the wilderness of the stream, but now it knew it was on a journey within the wilderness of the soul.

For it was not a salmon, but a teardrop returning to the infinite sea of divine consciousness. And as it moved to where the stream meets the sea, the steady thumping again came into its awareness, growing louder until it drowned out the sound of the rushing water.

Eventually, the I Am was in darkness, and it began to feel as if it were floating, and time seemed to stretch for an eternity. As it exhaled, it felt an expansiveness - a connection to all things. And it did not know where it had ended, and where everything else had begun, for through its breath it felt it and the universe were one. For the first time since it had begun its long journey up river, it felt at peace.

Suddenly, it felt squeezed, then within the darkness appeared a light. And the I Am moved toward the brightness. And when the crown of its head emerged, it suddenly felt the coldness of the air against its skin. Overwhelmed by the many sensations of this new world, it cried, frightened, hearing sounds which it had not experienced before. Then it felt the warmth and softness of flesh against its skin, and it was soothed by a gentle and familiar voice. As it was being held, it gazed into its own eyes. And the I Am had forgotten itself.

Are You Willing to Empower Young Adults?

Thank you for reading *I Am*. Your support helps the book gain more exposure and touch the lives of young people. If you found the book meaningful, you can help spread the word by:

1) Giving it a 5 star rating on Amazon or Good Reads and writing a few words in a review.

2) Purchasing copies for friends and family. It's a great gift!

3) Sharing it on social media.

Like me on Facebook: @transcendencepress
Follow me on Instagram: transcendencepress

More Books by Corey Wolff

The Journey of An Acorn

Mikey McMonsterson Goes to School

www.ingramcontent.com/pod-product-compliance
Lightning Source LLC
Chambersburg PA
CBHW040543170726
48295CB00012B/577